This edition first published in the United States and Canada in 2017
by NorthSouth Books Inc., an imprint of NordSüd Verlag AG, CH-8005, Zürich, Switzerland.
Distributed in the United States by NorthSouth Books Inc., New York 10016.

Library of Congress Cataloging-in-Publication Data is available.
ISBN: 978-0-7358-4277-9

Printed in Latvia by Livonia Print, Riga, August 2016.
1 3 5 7 9 • 10 8 6 4 2
www.northsouth.com

FSC
www.fsc.org
MIX
Paper from
responsible sources
FSC® C104723

The Adventures of Pettson and Findus
The Camping Trip

Sven Nordqvist

North
South

Old man Pettson was up in his attic looking for a bag of fishing bobbers. His cat, Findus, was helping him as usual. As Pettson rummaged through a box, Findus saw a green sausage—a big, green sausage made of cloth. He jumped on top of it and balanced. When he walked forward, it rolled backward, and when he walked backward, it rolled forward. When he ran, it rolled faster.

"Hey, Pettson," he exclaimed, "check this out!"

Pettson looked up from his box and said, "Oh, I see. Hey, be careful! Watch out that you don't roll down the . . ."

"Helllllp!"

The sausage thudded down the stairs with the cat flailing along behind.

"Findus, are you okay?" Pettson asked, hurrying down after him.

"Yeaaaah," whined the cat. "I think I broke my ear. Why do you keep such dangerous sausages lying around the attic?" he scolded.

"It's a tent," Pettson said.

"What do you mean a *tent*?" Findus asked. "What's a tent?"

"It's a house made out of cloth that you can sleep in if you're hiking in the mountains, for instance."

The cat stared at the old man as if he was nuts.

"You're supposed to sleep in this while you're hiking? What, do you walk while you're asleep or something? With this sausage on your head?"

"No, no," Pettson said patiently. "There's a rolled-up tent inside this bag. Here, I'll show you."

Pettson pulled the tent out of the bag and unfolded it. The smell of it reminded him so vividly of how it felt to sleep in the tent, even though he hadn't done it in ages. How much fun they'd had when he was young! What if he was to try it again? Then he could test out his new invention.

Findus found the door and crawled inside.

"I want to sleep in here," he said. "Couldn't we go hiking in the mountains? Wait, what are mountains?"

"They're like really big hills," Pettson said.

"Hey, we have a really big hill out behind the toolshed," Findus said. "We could go hiking there."

"Well, that wouldn't be much of a hike," Pettson said. "That would only take fifteen minutes."

"But, Pettson, we don't *need* much of a hike. We could just go for a little walk and then sleep in the tent!"

"But I want to try out my invention," Pettson said. "Why don't we go for a long walk, all the way around the lake? We can stop and camp halfway around. We can go fishing and then sit by the lake while the sun sets and grill some perch over the campfire."

"Yes!" cried Findus, running outside. "We're doing that. Come on, let's go!"

"Hold your horses. I have to pack a few things first."

Tent, sleeping bag, backpack, coffeepot, the invention, which wasn't quite done . . . It took a long time to decide what to bring and track it all down.

The cat waited impatiently.

Finally they were on their way. As they walked past some of the chickens, Findus yelled, "Bye, chickens! We're going hiking in the mountains and camping and fishing in the lake and you can't come."

"Why can't we come?" clucked the hens, running after them. "Pettson, we want to camp by the lake, too!"

"No, that won't work," Pettson said. "You can't walk that far. You'll just get lost in the woods and then the fox will come eat you up. You have to stay here!"

"We're coming!" squawked the hens.

Pettson broke into a run, but the hens ran after him.

Old Mrs. Andersson was out tending her beets and saw Pettson running from the hens.

"Don't be scared, Pettson!" she called out. "They're just chickens. They're not as dangerous as they look!"

Pettson stopped. This was just getting too silly. The hens had to go back home.

He went back, and the hens followed him skeptically. He went over to the chicken run and called to them, "Come here, little chicks, time for bed now! Here, chicky, chicky!"

Findus ran around trying to herd them in, but of course that didn't work.

They clucked, "He thinks we're stupid! *Brock*! It's the middle of the day! If you're going camping by the lake, Pettson, we're coming. If you're staying here, so are we."

Their message was clear. That was how it was going to be.

There was just no persuading ten hens.

"We'll go hiking some other time,
Findus," Pettson said. "Anyway,
now you won't have to walk so far."
Findus was disappointed. He
bounced around scolding the hens.
But then Pettson said they
could set up the tent
in the yard instead,
and everyone was happy
again. The cat helped
and the hens watched and
soon the tent was up.

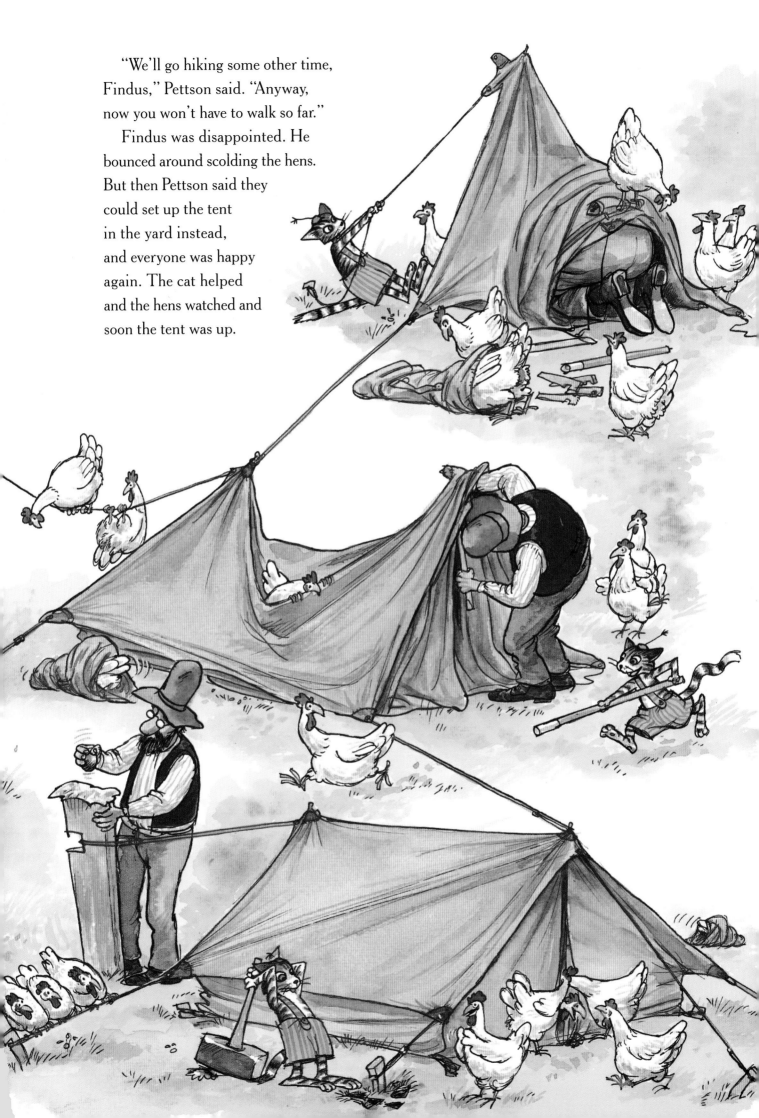

Pettson rolled out the sleeping bag, and Findus crawled in. The cat looked pleased and announced, "This is a perfect house for me. I'm going to sleep in here tonight."

"We're going to sleep here tonight, too," clucked the hens.

"No, you can't!" squealed Findus. "They can't, right, Pettson?"

"I'm sure it will all work out," the old man said. "Come here, Findus. I need your help with something."

When they were out of earshot of the hens, Pettson whispered, "Let them be. They'll be tired soon. In the meantime we can go fishing. I want to try out my new invention."

Pettson had invented a fishing bow. The hook and the bobber were attached to the front of the arrow. The back of the arrow was attached to the fishing line. The rest of the line was wound around a reel that was attached to the bow. This way he could shoot the arrow and the fishhook way out into the water, much farther than he could have just using a rod. It worked really well.

Pettson aimed at a clump of reeds way out in the lake. He was sure there were big pike out there. For a long time nothing happened, other than Findus catching one perch after another from where he stood on a rock fishing the normal way.

Then Pettson took the smallest perch and put it on his hook as bait and shot it off. The arrow had scarcely landed in the water when there was a splash. It was a whopping splash from a whopper of a fish.

"Findus?" Pettson squeaked. "Did you see that? What a pike!"

It was as big as a seal. It broke the surface again. Pettson held onto his bow for all he was worth, then the line snapped and vanished into the lake after the fish.

The old man and the cat watched in silence until the ripples faded and the lake was smooth again.

"Well, I'll be," Pettson whispered. "I've never seen one that big before."

"We're going home now," Findus announced, darting away from the lake. "Come on, Pettson! We have plenty of fish."

On the way back, Findus wanted to know all about how big and dangerous pike could get. But Pettson was very quiet and lost in thought, and hardly answered. For as long as the lake was visible he kept turning around and looking back at that clump of reeds, but the lake was still.

When they got back, sure enough, the hens had grown tired of being in the tent. May-Rose was the only one still in the sleeping bag laying eggs.

Pettson built a campfire on the gravel path and made a pot of coffee. Then they grilled the perch over the coals and pretended they were in the mountains. Pettson leaned against the apple tree and breathed a deep sigh.

"Ahh, nothing beats grilled perch and a cup of coffee after a long day of hiking in the mountains; that's what I hear anyway."

"You mean you don't know?" Findus said.

"Nope. I've never actually been to the mountains. We just never made it there. We didn't have time for that sort of thing, and we couldn't afford it either. But it sure would have been fun."

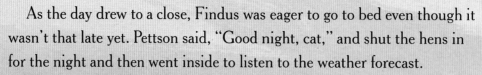

As the day drew to a close, Findus was eager to go to bed even though it wasn't that late yet. Pettson said, "Good night, cat," and shut the hens in for the night and then went inside to listen to the weather forecast.

Findus lay by himself in the tent. It was exciting. In a tent the light was different and so was the dark. The sounds were all different in the tent, too. He could actually hear every little whisper and rustle more clearly.

Since he couldn't see, he worked twice as hard to figure out what was making each sound. No matter how hard he listened, he wasn't sure what he was hearing. What sound did giant pike make, anyway?

Suddenly being alone in a tent was a little bit too exciting. He jumped out of the sleeping bag, peeked out of the tent flap, and then ran as fast as he could to the kitchen, to Pettson.

The old man was just on his way to bed when the cat darted inside.

"What is it?" said Pettson. "Wasn't it fun sleeping in the tent?"

"Yeah," said Findus. "It was fun for a long time, but then it got so lonely. I think it would be more fun if there were two of us."

"Oh, really?" said Pettson. "I didn't think you were scared of the dark."

"The thing is, when you're lying in a tent, you can hear so much more," said Findus. "Which is why I thought that if you sat out there with me, I wouldn't hear so much, and then sleeping in the tent would be a lot more fun."

"All right, sure," mumbled Pettson. "We'll see how it goes."

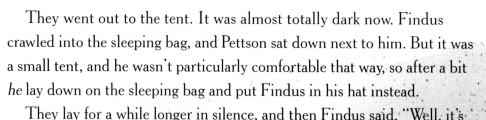

They went out to the tent. It was almost totally dark now. Findus
crawled into the sleeping bag, and Pettson sat down next to him. But it was
a small tent, and he wasn't particularly comfortable that way, so after a bit
he lay down on the sleeping bag and put Findus in his hat instead.

They lay for a while longer in silence, and then Findus said, "Well, it's
a good thing you didn't catch that pike today. It would probably have eaten
us. Next time you go fishing I don't think I'm going to go."

"You don't need to be afraid," Pettson said. "I've never seen anything that
big before, so I'm sure we'll probably never see it again. Now go to sleep."

And then he fell asleep—Pettson, that is.

And before Findus realized he was alone again, he was asleep, too.

Findus woke up early in the morning, before it was even really light out. He was cold and thirsty, so he ran into the house and drank a little milk. Then he went to Pettson's bedroom and took the time to do a little jumping on the bed, because the old man didn't like it when he saw that; but he wasn't here now to see it, was he? Then it was so warm and comfy under the covers that he lay down for a while. Just for a little while, before he went back to the tent.

Although, why did he need to go back to the tent, anyway? He might as well stay here and be comfortable.

Findus woke up when the biggest pike in the world knocked on the door. Half asleep, he jumped up and listened. The kitchen door opened, and the pike came inside, calling out, "Hello? Pettson! Are you awake? It's your neighbor, Gustavsson."

Findus kept quiet. He didn't like Gustavsson. He jumped out the window and ran to the tent and woke up Pettson.

Before the old man was fully awake, Gustavsson peeked into the tent.

"Hello there, Pettson. It's eight o'clock. Rise and shine!"

Pettson grunted and started struggling to crawl out of the tent.

"So, you're . . . camping," Gustavsson said. "Are you on vacation?"

Pettson was embarrassed that his neighbor had caught him sleeping in a tent in the yard. Grown-ups didn't usually do that.

"Well, not exactly," he mumbled. He wasn't sure what to say. "Uh, it wasn't me. . . . It was Findus."

"Oh, I see," Gustavsson said, rubbing his chin. "It was Findus, huh? Sure looks like you, though. Same hat anyway."

From the smile on Gustavsson's face, Pettson could tell that by the end of the day all the neighbors were going to know that kooky old Pettson had been out camping in his own yard.

Suddenly Pettson felt annoyed.

"I appreciate that you need some news to tell the neighbors," he said. "So let me tell you what's really been going on. Findus and I went hiking in the mountains for a few days. We were up in Lapland by Mount Sulitjelma when a pack of white wolves chased us and we got lost. We wound up by Lake Torne and went fishing. I caught a deep-sea monster with my bow and arrow, but threw it back. Findus caught a few salmon. Then we came home and ate them, and I was so full that I dozed off. Then I woke up in the tent. Findus must have set up the tent around me. While I was sleeping. Isn't that right, Findus?"

The cat nodded.

"So, you see, that's what happened," Pettson said. "I hope you don't have any objections to me taking a little catnap in my own yard?"

"No, no," Gustavsson said, "not at all." He seemed completely flummoxed. He didn't know what to think. "I just stopped by to borrow a pipe wrench," he added.

They strolled over to the toolshed. Gustavsson got his wrench and went home, still at a bit of a loss for words.

"You can borrow the tent, too," Pettson called after him. "If you're taking the family on vacation. Actually, take the cows, too. They could stand to get out a little!"

Gustavsson didn't respond.

"Why did you tell him that whole made-up story?" Findus asked.

"Well, if he's going to go around gossiping, he might as well have a good story to tell. I mean, there's really not much to say about someone camping in their yard."

"Hey, Pettson, you know what?" Findus said. "We forgot to go hiking in the mountains."

"True. Well, why don't we do it now? We can go up that mountain behind the toolshed and have breakfast."

"Yes! Let's do it! Come on, Pettson, we're going!"

Backyard Camping Checklist

The Basics:
- A nice evening (spring, summer, or fall)
- A good friend or a parent to join you! (Hens are optional)
- Tent (or blanket, sheet, or tarp draped over a rope or tree branch. Rocks or stakes can help hold down the corners)
- Pillow
- Sleeping bag (or a sheet with blankets/comforter)
- Sleeping pad (air mattress or blanket to make it more comfortable if ground is rocky)
- Layered clothing which can be easily removed or added depending on the weather
- Hats (if the weather is chilly)
- Bug spray
- Flashlights (preferably one for each person)

Snacks:
- Clean water to drink (jug of water and cups)
- Snacks (apples, carrots, peanut butter, popcorn or marshmallows, graham crackers, chocolate bars for raw or cooked s'mores)
- Napkins, paper plates, cups, and plastic forks if needed
- Trash bag

For fun:
- Song book or instruments to play
- Games, crayons, paper, cards, or a good book to read aloud
- Camera
- Magnifying glass and binoculars
- Field guide to animals, insects, birds, stars, etc.
- A good sense of humor!

Be sure to check out the first three books in the series!

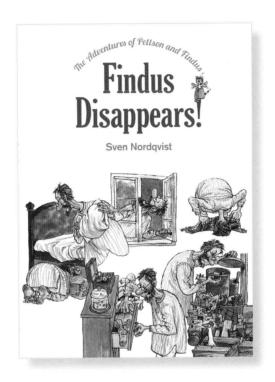

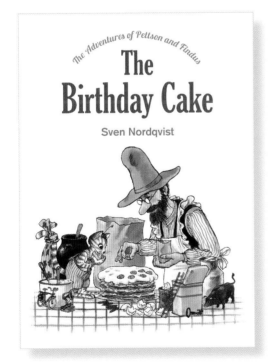

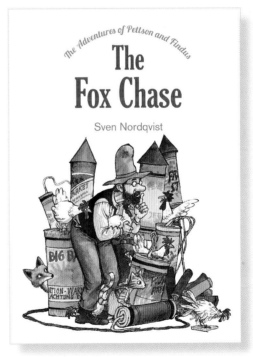